MW01252385

BODY WORKS™

NERVES

The Nervous System

Gillian Houghton

PowerKiDS
press

New York

Published in 2007 by The Rosen Publishing Group, Inc.
29 East 21st Street, New York, NY 10010

First Edition

Editor: Amelie von Zumbusch
Book Design: Greg Tucker

Photo Credits: Cover © 3D4Medical.com/Getty Images; p. 5 © Paul Singh-Roy/Photo Researchers, Inc.; pp. 6 (left),13, 14 (right), 18 (right) © Anatomical Travelogue/Photo Researchers, Inc.; p. 6 (right) © Norbert Schaefer/Corbis; p. 9 © Mike Chew/Corbis; p. 10 (top) © Creasource/Corbis; p. 10 (bottom) © Pascal Goetgheluck/Photo Researchers, Inc.; p. 14 (left) © SPL/Photo Researchers, Inc; p. 17 (left) © John M. Daugherty / Photo Researchers, Inc; p. 17 (right) © Bo Veisland, MI&I/Photo Researchers, Inc; p. 18 (left) © John Bavosi/Photo Researchers, Inc; p. 21 (left) © Chuck Savage/Corbis; p. 21 (right) © Fotex/Custom Medical Stock Photo.

Library of Congress Cataloging-in-Publication Data

Houghton, Gillian.
  Nerves : the nervous system / Gillian Houghton.
      p. cm. — (Body works)
  Includes index.
  ISBN (10) 1-4042-3474-8 (13) 978-1-4042-3474-1 (library binding) — ISBN (10) 1-4042-2183-2 (13) 978-1-4042-2183-3 (pbk.)
  1. Nervous system—Juvenile literature. I. Title. II. Human body systems (New York, N.Y.)
  QP361.5.H68 2007
  612.8—dc22
                                        2006000737

Manufactured in the United States of America

Contents

The Nervous System ————————

  All the body's systems are tied together and directed by the nervous system. The body uses the nervous system to move **information** from one place to another. The nervous system is like the web of telephone lines that reaches across North America. Instead of carrying sound over cables, the nervous system carries **electrical impulses** along **nerve** cells called neurons. Some impulses pass along information gathered from nerves throughout the body. Other impulses carry directions to **muscles** and **organs** that tell them how to respond to, or deal with, this new information.

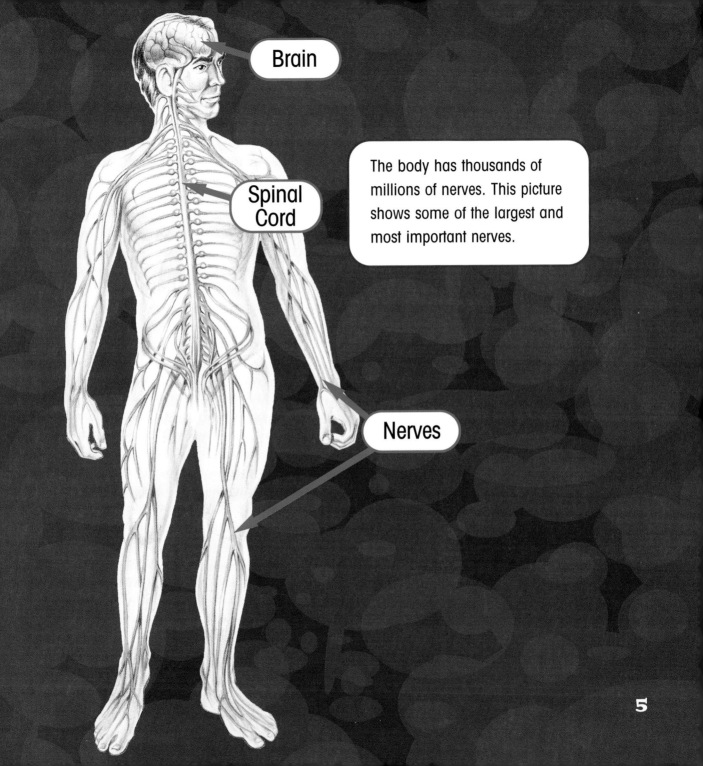

Brain

Spinal Cord

Nerves

The body has thousands of millions of nerves. This picture shows some of the largest and most important nerves.

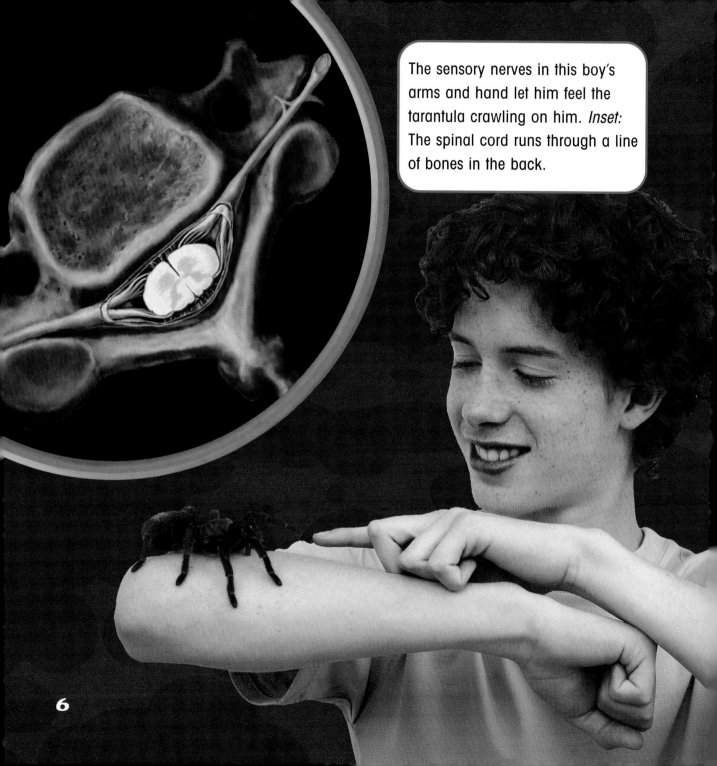

The sensory nerves in this boy's arms and hand let him feel the tarantula crawling on him. *Inset:* The spinal cord runs through a line of bones in the back.

6

The Parts of the Nervous System

The nervous system is made up of the central nervous system and the **peripheral** nervous system. The central nervous system acts as the body's command center. It is made up of the **brain** and the **spinal cord**. The central nervous system controls how the body responds to each change it faces.

The peripheral nervous system is a web of nerves that reaches throughout the body. The **sensory** nerves carry information from the sense organs to the central nervous system. The motor nerves carry directions from the central nervous system to the muscles and organs.

A Healthy Body

The nervous system responds to changes that come from both the outside world and inside the body. The nervous system controls the work of all the organs. For example, the nervous system controls how fast we breathe. It makes sure the body does not get too hot or too cold. It also sets the rate at which the heart beats.

The nervous system does these and many other jobs in order to keep the body in a state of **homeostasis**. Homeostasis happens when every part of the body is working well together.

The nervous system makes sure that every part of the body works well together. This makes it possible for people to do things like riding a bike or snowboarding.

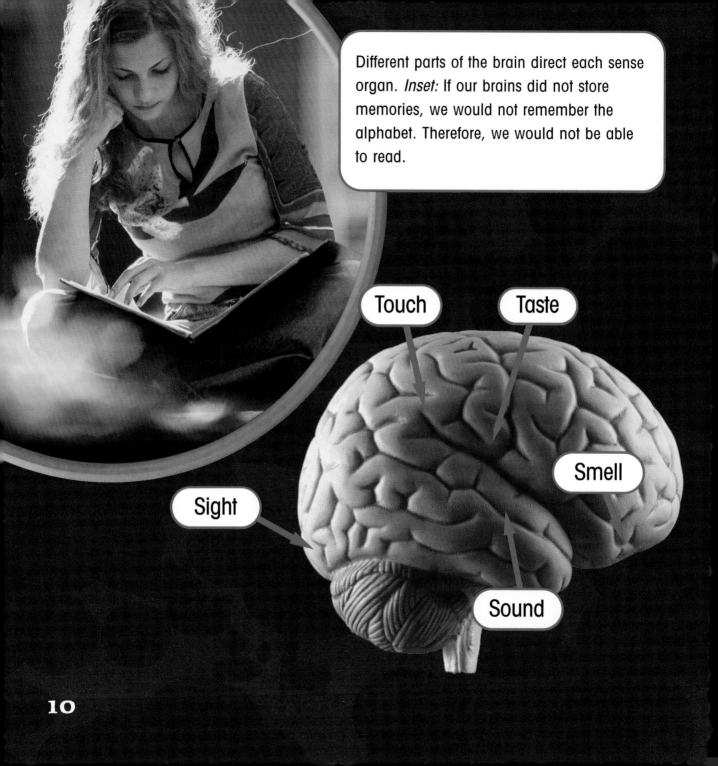

Different parts of the brain direct each sense organ. *Inset:* If our brains did not store memories, we would not remember the alphabet. Therefore, we would not be able to read.

Touch

Taste

Smell

Sight

Sound

Sense and Memory

Your eyes, ears, nose, and skin are all sense organs. This means they take in information from the world around you. A different part of the brain controls each sense organ. The brain sorts through the information from the sense organs and stores this information as **memories**.

If our brains could not store memories, we would not be able to learn. We could not use memories of our past actions to escape danger and seek out safety. We learn to respond to the world around us by building our stores of memories.

The Brain

The brain is a large organ in the head. The largest part of the brain is the cerebrum. Different parts of the **cerebrum** control different things. These parts are called centers. There are centers for movement, writing, reading, speech, and memory. Other centers receive sensory information, such as tastes, sights, and sounds.

A part of the brain called the **cerebellum** allows the body to make smooth, even movements. The pons helps direct sensory information. The **medulla oblongata** plays a part in breathing and the flow of blood through the body.

Cerebrum

Thalamus

Hippocampus

Pons

Medulla
Oblongata

Cerebellum

The thalamus passes information from the sense organs to the cerebrum. The hippocampus is a part of the brain that stores memories.

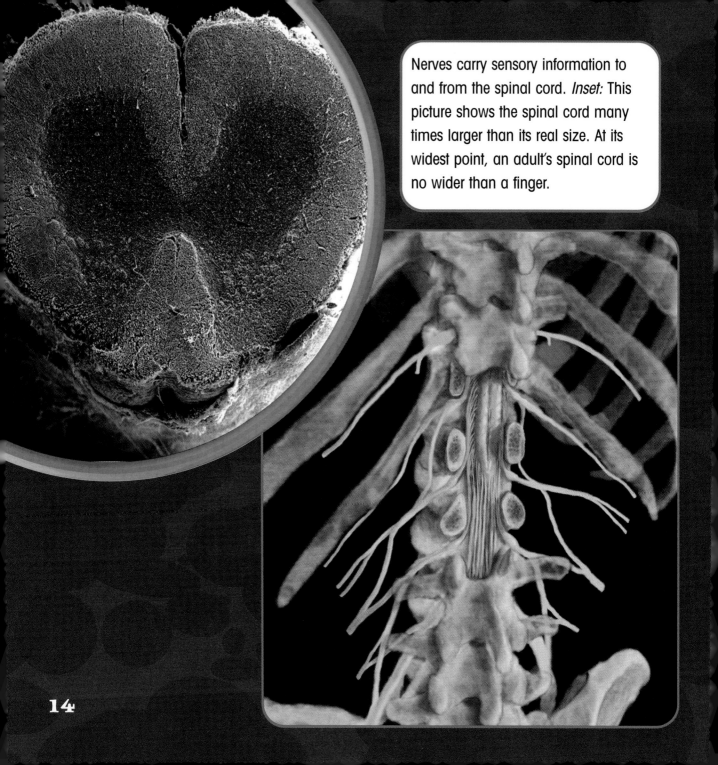

Nerves carry sensory information to and from the spinal cord. *Inset:* This picture shows the spinal cord many times larger than its real size. At its widest point, an adult's spinal cord is no wider than a finger.

The Spinal Cord

The spinal cord is a thick, white group of nerves. It lies inside a tunnel-like group of bones in the center of the back called the spine. The spinal cord ties the brain to the rest of the body. It begins at the bottom of the medulla oblongata and ends in the lower back.

The neurons that carry sensory information end at the center of the spinal cord. The neurons carrying motor directions begin there. These two kinds of neurons are tied together by a special kind of nerve cell.

The Peripheral Nervous System

The peripheral nervous system is made up of the nerves that branch out from the central nervous system. The most important of these are the 31 pairs of spinal nerves. They branch out from the spinal cord to the organs and muscles throughout the body. **Blood vessels** run alongside each nerve. They supply the nerve cells with the blood they need to do their work.

Most nerves are like two-way roads. They are able to pass along both sensory information and motor directions along side-by-side lines of nerve cells.

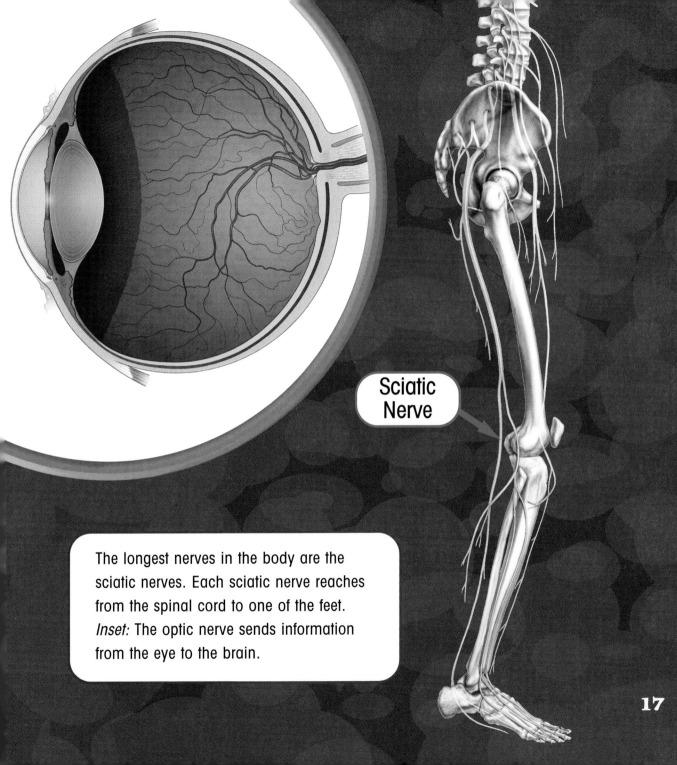

Sciatic
Nerve

The longest nerves in the body are the
sciatic nerves. Each sciatic nerve reaches
from the spinal cord to one of the feet.
Inset: The optic nerve sends information
from the eye to the brain.

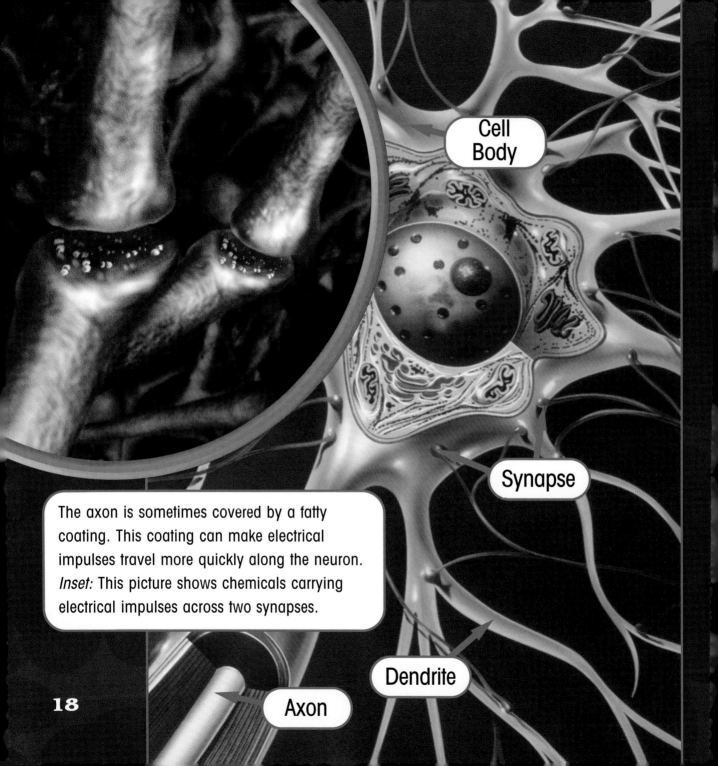

Cell Body

Synapse

The axon is sometimes covered by a fatty coating. This coating can make electrical impulses travel more quickly along the neuron. *Inset:* This picture shows chemicals carrying electrical impulses across two synapses.

Dendrite

Axon

The Neuron

Each nerve is made of thousands of neurons and the cells that keep them safe. Each neuron has a round cell body covered with fingerlike **dendrites** and one long axon. Neurons are strung together, with the **axon** of one neuron nearly touching the next neuron's dendrites.

There is a small space called a synapse between one neuron's axon and the next neuron's dendrites. When an electrical impulse is made, the axon gives off a **chemical** that carries the impulse across the synapse. The impulse moves along the neuron and down its axon.

Taking Action

The central nervous system sorts through information and responds to it. Some of these responses are voluntary, or something you decide to do. For example, when you see a friend, you might decide to say hello.

Other actions are reflexes, which means you do them without thinking about them. For example, when you touch something hot, you pull your hand away very quickly. Reflexes are usually controlled by the spinal cord. It takes less time for an impulse to reach the spinal cord than it would take for it to reach the brain.

The knee-jerk reaction is a reflex. When a spot below a person's knee is hit, that person's leg suddenly jerks, or kicks out. *Inset:* Reaching out and deciding which CD to pick is a voluntary action.

21

Problems of the Nervous System

Many diseases, or illnesses, hurt the nervous system. Parkinson's disease destroys the parts of the brain that control movement. Stroke is a **circulatory system** disease that hurts the brain. During a stroke the blood flowing to part of the brain becomes blocked. Neurons in that part of the brain die. The senses, movements, or memories controlled by these neurons no longer work.

Eating healthy foods and exercising helps makes people less likely to have a stroke. Exercising your brain, by doing things such as figuring out riddles or playing music, is good for your memory.

Glossary

axon (AK-son) The long part of a neuron that passes along impulses.

blood vessels (BLUD VEH-suhlz) Narrow tunnels in the body, through which blood flows.

brain (BRAYN) The soft body part found in the head that allows thought, movement, and feeling.

cerebellum (ser-eh-BEH-lum) A part of the brain that controls movement.

cerebrum (seh-REE-brem) The largest part of the brain. It helps with memory and thought.

chemical (KEH-mih-kul) Matter that can be mixed with other matter to cause changes.

circulatory system (SER-kyuh-luh-tor-ee SIS-tehm) The path by which blood travels through the body.

dendrites (DEN-dryts) The parts of a neuron that receive impulses from other neurons.

electrical impulses (ih-LEK-trih-kul IM-puls-ez) Cues that neurons uses to send messages to one another.

homeostasis (hom-mee-oh-STAY-sus) A state in which every part of the body is working together.

information (in-fer-MAY-shun) Knowledge or facts.

medulla oblongata (meh-DUH-luh oh-blon-GOH-tuh) The part of the brain that controls things like breathing and the flow of blood.

memories (MEM-reez) Facts that are remembered.

muscles (MUH-sulz) Parts of the body that are used to make the body move.

nerve (NERV) Having to do with a group of cells that carry messages between the brain and other parts of the body.

organs (OR-genz) Parts inside the body that do a job.

peripheral (puh-RIH-fuh-rul) Not in the center.

sensory (SENS-ree) Having to do with the senses.

spinal cord (SPY-nul KORD) A long bundle of tissue that runs down the back and that carries messages between the brain the rest of the body.

Index

Web Sites

Due to the changing nature of Internet links, PowerKids Press has developed an online list of Web sites related to the subject of this book. This site is updated regularly. Please use this link to access the list: www.powerkidslinks.com/hybw/nervous/